Dinosaurs in the Supermarket

By Timothy Knapman

Illustrated by Sarah Warburton

SCHOLASTIC

There are **dinosaurs** in the **supermarket**!
Look, they're everywhere!
If only grown-ups noticed them
They'd get a frightful scare.

Dinosaurs in the Supermarket

STEGOSAURUS
(STEG-oh-SORE-us)

PTEROSAUR
(TERR-oh-sore)

HADROSAURUS
(HAD-row-SORE-us)

IGUANODON
(ig-WHA-noh-don)

TRICERATOPS
(tri-SERRA-tops)

To Michael and Edward, with love
T.K.

For Lucy and Harry
S.W.

First published in 2013 by Scholastic Children's Books
Euston House, 24 Eversholt Street
London NW1 1DB
a division of Scholastic Ltd
www.scholastic.co.uk
London ~ New York ~ Toronto ~ Sydney ~ Auckland
Mexico City ~ New Delhi ~ Hong Kong

Text copyright © 2013 Timothy Knapman
Illustrations copyright © 2013 Sarah Warburton
HB ISBN 978 1 407 11472 9
PB ISBN 978 1 407 11471 2
All rights reserved
Printed in Malaysia

13 15 17 19 20 18 16 14

The moral rights of Timothy Knapman and Sarah Warburton have been asserted.

Papers used by Scholastic Children's Books are made from wood grown in sustainable forests.

There's T. rex gobbling sausages...

Stegosaurus spilling beans...

Apatosaurs chucking frozen peas
Are filling the aisles with greens!

There are dinosaurs in the supermarket!
But when I tell my mum
They hide until she looks away...

And then...right back they come!

Ankylosaurus and his trolley
Crash into all those cans.
The pterosaurs go flying
And end up in the flans!

Triceratops squirt chocolate sauce.
Hadrosaurs scoff cake.
Iguanodons chuck toilet rolls.
What a MONSTER MESS they make!

"Our supermarket's ruined!"
The check-out staff despair.
"The car park's full of ice cream,
And there's ketchup everywhere!"

"There are DINOSAURS in the supermarket!"
I shout out straight away.
"Look, their custard footprints
Must be clear as day!"

"DINOSAURS in the SUPERMARKET?
Please don't have us on!"

I point to where I saw them...

...But the dinosaurs have gone.

If this goes on much longer,
They'll think that I'm to blame.
So I find those sneaky dinosaurs
And say, "Let's play a game...

...called Supermarket Clean-up."
I give each one a mop.
They plunge them in the suds and – SPLAT!
They splash and swoosh and slop!

In no time, things are shining bright.
The grown-ups say, "Well done!
This boy here cleaned the supermarket."
My mum says, "That's my son!"

But I DIDN'T. It was DINOSAURS!
They don't believe it's true...

...Till hordes of soapy dinosaurs
Jump out, shouting... "BOO!"

STEGOSAURUS
(STEG-oh-SORE-us)

PTEROSAUR
(TERR-oh-sore)

HADROSAURUS
(HAD-row-SORE-us)

IGUANODON
(ig-WHA-noh-don)

TRICERATOPS
(tri-SERRA-tops)

ANKYLOSAURUS
(an-KIE-loh-sore-us)

TYRANNOSAURUS REX
(tie-RAN-oh-sore-us rex)

APATOSAURUS
(ah-PAT-oh-sore-us)

Splat!